Dedicated to Tracy, xxx
- Vince

This book is given with love to...

_____

_____

Copyright © 2021 by Vince Cleghorne.
All rights reserved. Published in the United States
by Puppy Dogs & Ice Cream, Inc.
ISBN: 978-1-956462-29-6
Edition: September 2021

PDIC and PUPPY DOGS & ICE CREAM are trademarks of
Puppy Dogs & Ice Cream, Inc.

For all inquiries, please contact us at:
info@puppysmiles.org

To see more of our books, visit us at:
www.PuppyDogsAndIceCream.com

Cock-a-Doodle Rooster was in charge of all the chickens on Farmer's ranch.

Having one of the biggest jobs on the farm, Cock-a-Doodle thought he was more important than the rest of the animals. Because of this, he was not very nice to be around.

"My heated rooster house is the size of a barn because I'm important!" he'd say to Pig.

"I have the softest bed on the farm because I'm important!" he'd say to Sheep.

"I can insult anyone I please and call them names because I'm important, Rump-steak!" he'd say to Cow.

One freezing cold day, while Cock-a-Doodle was inside his heated rooster house and snug in his soft bed, Pig arrived at the window and shouted, "Cock-a-Doodle! I hear Farmer's having chicken noodle soup for dinner!"

"Big deal!" said Cock-a-Doodle. "There are lots of chickens on this farm."

"All the chickens have been taken to the market," said Pig. "That means you're going in the soup!"

"COCK-A-DOODLE-DOO! Say it isn't true!" crowed Cock-a-Doodle.

"It's true!" said Pig. "But I know how you can stop Farmer from having chicken noodle soup for dinner."

"Oh, please tell me, Pig old pal," begged Cock-a-Doodle.

"When you see Farmer, wiggle your bottom as fast as you can," said Pig. "But why?" Cock-a-Doodle asked.

"When Farmer sees your bottom wiggling, he'll be reminded of how huge his own bottom is and he'll skip dinner to lose a little weight."

"Thanks, Bacon-face!" laughed Cock-a-Doodle as he dashed off to find Farmer.

Cock-a-Doodle ran across the farmyard and straight into Sheep.

"Where are you off to, Cock-a-Doodle?" Sheep asked.

"I'm going to wiggle my bottom so Farmer won't have chicken noodle soup for dinner!" said Cock-a-Doodle.

"Wiggling your bottom won't stop Farmer from having chicken noodle soup for dinner," said Sheep.

"It might even make him think of the noodles wiggling in the pan and give him more of an appetite."

"COCK-A-DOODLE-DOO! Say it isn't true!" crowed Cock-a-Doodle.

"It's true!" said Sheep. "But I know what else you can do to stop Farmer from having chicken noodle soup for dinner."

"Oh, please tell me, Sheep old chum," begged Cock-a-Doodle.

"After you wiggle your bottom, do lots and lots of cartwheels," said Sheep.

"But why?" Cock-a-Doodle asked.

"When Farmer sees you doing cartwheels, he'll get so dizzy that he won't feel like cooking dinner."

"Thanks, Wool-head!" laughed Cock-a-Doodle as he dashed off to find Farmer.

Cock-a-Doodle ran to the farmhouse but was stopped at the gate by Cow.

"Where are you off to, Cock-a-Doodle?" Cow asked. "I'm off to wiggle my bottom and do cartwheels so Farmer won't have chicken noodle soup for dinner!" said Cock-a-Doodle.

"Wiggling your bottom and doing cartwheels won't stop Farmer from having chicken noodle soup for dinner," said Cow. "You might even remind him to put on the TV show he watches while eating dinner, The Wiggling Cartwheel Show."

"COCK-A-DOODLE-DOO! Say it isn't true!" crowed Cock-a-Doodle.

"It's true!" said Cow. "But I know what else you can do to stop Farmer from having chicken noodle soup for dinner."

"Oh, please tell me, Cow old buddy," begged Cock-a-Doodle.

"After you wiggle your bottom and do your cartwheels, hit Farmer with your wings over and over again," said Cow.

"But why?" Cock-a-Doodle asked.

"When Farmer sees your wings, he'll remember that his most favorite TV show, Wings of the Sky, is on the other channel. He'll switch channels and will forget to cook his dinner."

"Thanks, Beefburger-head!" laughed Cock-a-Doodle as he dashed off to find Farmer.

When Cock-a-Doodle spotted Farmer, he immediately ran over and...

Wiggled his bottom as fast as he could...

Did lots and lots of cartwheels...

And hit Farmer with his wings over and over again!

Farmer frowned, brushed the feathers from his face, and called to Mrs. Farmer: "I think we've been working this rooster a bit too hard, dear! I'll take him to the animal doctor. A sip of medicine and a few nights in a cold cage, and he should be fine!"

"I'll put your shepherd's pie in the oven for when you get back!" said Mrs. Farmer.

Cock-a-Doodle was puzzled. Shepherd's pie? What happened to chicken noodle soup?

Suddenly, Cock-a-Doodle realized that Pig, Sheep and Cow had tricked him. "Of course!" he thought.

They were getting back at him for all of the times he had teased them, for all the times he had bragged about his heated house and his soft bed when they were freezing cold, and for all the times he had called them names.

Farmer put Cock-a-Doodle in the sidecar of his motorbike and drove across the farm. Peeking out of the sidecar Cock-a-Doodle saw Pig, Sheep, and Cow curled up nice and warm in his luxury rooster house.

From that day on, Cock-a-Doodle became a much nicer rooster to be around. And whenever the weather got really cold, Cock-a-Doodle always invited Pig, Sheep, and Cow to sleep over.

Cock-a-Doodle finally realized how unfair he had been, and from that day he was never unfair again.

Cock-a-doodle-doo!
The End

Claim your FREE Gift!

Visit: PDICBooks.com/Gift

Thank you for purchasing
Cock-a-Doodle Chicken Noodle

and welcome to the Puppy Dogs & Ice Cream family. We're certain you're going to love the little gift we've prepared for you at the website above.

CPSIA information can be obtained
at www.ICGtesting.com
Printed in the USA
LVHW071951030122
707222LV00019B/28